Jellybean Books™

W9-DHI-012

Wait for ELMO!

by Molly Cross

illustrated by
Joe Mathieu

Featuring
Jim Henson's
Sesame Street Muppets

Random House/Children's Television Workshop

Copyright © 1987, 1998 Children's Television Workshop.
Jim Henson's Sesame Street Muppets copyright © 1987, 1998 The Jim Henson Company. All rights reserved.
Originally published in a different form under the title *Wait for Me!* as a Sesame Street Start-to-Read Book™.
First Random House Jellybean Books™ edition, 1998.   ISBN: 0-679-89190-0
http://www.randomhouse.com/   http://www.sesamestreet.com
JELLYBEAN BOOKS is a trademark of Random House, Inc.
Printed in the United States of America   10 9 8 7 6 5 4 3

Elmo was younger and smaller than all his friends on Sesame Street. It was hard for him to keep up with them because he couldn't run as fast or jump as far.

One sunny day, Ernie, Bert, Big Bird,
Grover, and Elmo went skating in the park.
They heard an ice cream truck's bell
jingling in the distance.

"Yay!" they shouted.
Ernie, Bert, Big Bird,
and Grover skated off
to get some ice cream.
"Hey!" Elmo cried.
"Wait for Elmo!"

Grover skated back to Elmo. "I, Grover, will
help you. I will pull you to the ice cream truck.
Hold my hand," he said.

Off they went.

Clickety-clack, lickety-split,
they raced faster and faster...

...until they hit a bump.
Crash! They fell down!

"Wah! Wah!" wailed Elmo.

"Oh my goodness! Are you hurt?" asked Grover.

"Elmo has a boo-boo!" Elmo cried.

Grover looked closely at Elmo's knee. At last he found a tiny scratch.

"Do not cry," said Grover.
"We are near my house.
We can go there
and wash your knee."

At Grover's house, Grover put a little
bandage on Elmo's knee. Then Grover
said he was going back to find
Ernie, Bert, and Big Bird.
"Elmo too?" asked Elmo.
"You are too little,
Elmo," replied Grover.
"Will Elmo be big
enough tomorrow?"
Elmo asked.
"I do not think
so," Grover
answered.

Elmo watched as Grover took his bike outside. He waved when Grover rode off. Grover waved back, but it didn't make Elmo feel any better.

"Everybody is bigger and faster than Elmo,"
Elmo said to himself.

"Not me!" said a kind voice.

It was Grover's grandpa!

"I know how you feel, Elmo," he said.
"But sometimes fun things happen even
when you are left behind. How would
you like to go to the zoo with me
this afternoon? I was going to ask
Grover, but he left in such a rush
that I didn't have a chance.
How about it, Elmo?"

Elmo smiled. "Oh yes!"

Elmo took Grandpa's hand and they walked to the zoo. Elmo didn't have to run to keep up. On the way they stopped to look in store windows and to buy ice cream cones. Then they stopped to listen to some musicians playing on a street corner.

"People who rush sometimes miss things," Grandpa said to Elmo. "We'll take our time and enjoy the day!"

At the zoo, they watched the zookeeper
feed fish to the seals.

Then Grandpa bought some peanuts and they fed them to the elephants.

After they saw all the animals, Grandpa and Elmo walked slowly home together.

As soon as they got home, Grandpa sat down in his chair and read Elmo a story.

Just then Grover burst through the door.

"Guess what!" said Elmo to Grover. "We went to the zoo!"

"You went to the zoo without me?"
Grover wailed.

"Grover, dear," said his Grandpa. "Did
you have fun bike riding with your friends?"

"Oh yes," said Grover.

"But, Grandpa, next time you go to the zoo, will you please wait for me?"